Surfing the net is fun — until your web crawler, Spyder, leaps out of your screen and sinks its fangs into you. Now a computer virus is erasing your memory so fast you can't even remember your own name!

It's going to be one fierce battle to save yourself. You might even have to go into virtual reality! Can you beat the ghouls from Coffin City? Can you outsmart the evil Digit Wizard?

And remember: If you get past all the rest, you'll still have to face Spyder — the creepiest crawler there is.

This scary adventure is about you. You decide what will happen — and how terrifying the scares will be!

Start on page 1. Then follow the instructions at the bottom of each page. You make the choices. If you choose well, you'll find a way to beat Spyder. But if you make the wrong choice . . . BEWARE!

SO TAKE A DEEP BREATH. CROSS YOUR FINGERS. AND TURN TO PAGE 1 NOW TO *GIVE YOURSELF GOOSEBUMPS!*

READER BEWARE —
YOU CHOOSE THE SCARE!

Look for more
GIVE YOURSELF GOOSEBUMPS adventures
from R.L. STINE:

R.L. STINE

GIVE YOURSELF

Goosebumps®

IT CAME FROM
THE INTERNET

AN
APPLE
PAPERBACK

SCHOLASTIC INC.
New York Toronto London Auckland Sydney
Mexico City New Delhi Hong Kong

A PARACHUTE PRESS BOOK

ISBN 0-590-51665-5

Copyright © 1999 by Parachute Press, Inc. All rights reserved. Published by Scholastic Inc. APPLE PAPERBACKS and associated logos are trademarks and/or registered trademarks of Scholastic Inc. GOOSEBUMPS is a registered trademark of Parachute Press, Inc.

12 11 10 9 8 7 6 5 4 3 2 1   9/9 0 1 2 3 4/0

Printed in the U.S.A.   40

First Scholastic printing, February 1999

"Tell me again," your best friend, Mark, demands. "You saw *what* on your computer screen?"

The hairs on the back of your neck prickle just thinking about it.

"A bump," you answer. "A weird, squirming bump. It stuck out of the monitor. Moved around like it was alive."

"Right." Mark rolls his eyes. "You're out of your mind!"

Mark talks tough, but you've known him since you were little. You're used to it.

"It's true," you insist. "And totally weird. Come on — see for yourself."

You slam the front door. Mark is already halfway up the stairs to your room when you catch up to him.

You turn on the computer and sit at your desk. With a couple of double-clicks and your password, you log on to the Internet.

"Okay, be prepared," you warn him. "It's pretty creepy."

"Like I care," Mark scoffs.

A moment later, a message pops up on your screen. A message in a little black box.

Mark's mouth drops open as he reads it.

Read the message on PAGE 2.

The message on your screen says:

EXPERIENCING VIRUS. NEED HELP TO AVOID FATAL ERROR.

"Oh, man!" Mark groans. "You've got a virus!"

"What's that?" you ask.

"You don't know what a computer virus is?" Mark stares at you in disbelief. "It's a program that gets into your computer and messes everything up. It can fry your whole hard drive."

You don't like the sound of that. "You mean, it could erase all my games and files and stuff?"

"Yup," Mark says. "Everything would just be . . . gone."

"Whoa," you say, sitting back from the screen a little bit.

Just then, your computer beeps. A long, loud, piercing beep. You cover your ears. Your eyes widen as the black message box doubles in size.

This time the message says:

PLEASE, I'M BEGGING YOU. HELP ME! THIS VIRUS IS REALLY BAD. I NEED HELP NOW. HURRY!

— YOUR WEB CRAWLER

Crawl over to PAGE 3.

You and Mark stare at the black message box on your screen.

A sick feeling hits your gut.

"Now, that's freaky," Mark says. "I never saw an error message like that. It sounds like a real person talking. Like it's alive."

You glance at Mark and shiver.

"What web crawler are you using, anyway?" Mark asks.

"It's called Spyder," you answer. You don't need to explain that a web crawler is a program you use to get around on the Internet. Mark knows. "Someone gave it to me for free," you add.

"Free software? Bad news!" Mark exclaims. "Free stuff always has viruses. Let's turn this off, reboot, and start over. Maybe the message will go away."

"Shouldn't we try to help the web crawler?" you ask.

"You decide. It's your computer," Mark says. "But I'll tell you this: If you try to fix it, you could totally crash your hard drive."

Hmmm, you think. Maybe he's right. . . .

But the web crawler *is* asking for help. . . .

To try to get rid of the virus, turn to PAGE 14.
If you don't dare mess with it, reboot on PAGE 43.

You decide to set the banana trap right there — in the Dot Com Diner. Mark hurries out to a nearby store to buy bananas.

"These cost me twenty bucks," he complains when he returns. "So this better work." He dumps a huge grocery bag of bananas onto the floor.

"Why did you buy so many?" Rachel asks. "The place stinks of bananas!"

"Hey," you tell her, "we don't know how many we need. He did great."

You grab a bunch of bananas and head toward the door. "Let's spread them everywhere. Under the couches. Near the computers . . ."

Suddenly there's a knock on the door of the Peach Pit. You jump.

"Now what?" Rachel grumbles as she opens the door. "Everyone knows they should leave me alone when I'm in here."

YIKES!

There's a gorilla outside the door! He's so big, he blocks the whole doorway. He must weigh three hundred pounds!

Face the gorilla on PAGE 58.

You feel a burst of excitement. Digit Wizard is Rachel's friend — the one who might be able to save your life!

"We've been looking for you everywhere," Rachel tells him. "You won't believe it, but this kid was bitten by a web crawler named Spyder. Now he has a computer virus! We need that antidote program of yours."

Digit Wizard shoots you a look of pity.

"I don't know if my program will help," he says. "That Spyder virus is bad news. It's a real killer."

A killer? Is he serious?

Find out if there's a cure on PAGE 109.

You follow Rachel into the graveyard — but you're not happy about it.

"Run! Faster!" Rachel calls, waving her arms for you to keep up. "The empty graves are over there!"

She dashes down the middle of a long row of gravestones. The ground around the graves bulges up.

"Ignore it," Rachel calls. "The corpses underneath are programmed to toss and turn in their graves. It's just part of the game."

Some game! You close your eyes. But it's pretty hard to run that way. You stumble and fall to one knee.

Then something reaches out and grabs you by the ankle.

Uh-oh.

Learn more about your grave situation on PAGE 15.

Of course not. Why would you want to hurt a fellow web crawler?

Spydie scampers across the kitchen floor, toward the hall.

"Where are you going?" you call after it.

"Up to your room," it says. "I can't wait to tell my buddies you're ready."

"Buddies?" you ask, feeling puzzled. "Ready?"

"Ready to crawl the Internet," it replies. "At the Goofy-humans website!" it says. "Bring your friend."

You suddenly remember Mark. You take his arm. Both of you follow Spydie into your room.

It hops up on your desk. Then it leaps onto the computer screen.

You hear a weird sucking noise.

THWAP. Spydie crawls back into the monitor.

"Follow me!" it yells.

Can you do that?

Find out on PAGE 55.

Every part of your body shakes as you tiptoe toward the dining room. You carefully peek around the corner.

And gag.

It's the Spyder all right. So ugly. So disgusting.

The worst part is the way it eats the bananas. Sucking them out of their skins whole. Slobbering.

"Oh," you whisper. "That yucky yellow stuff around its mouth? That's not pus. It's banana mush!"

The Spyder freezes when it hears your voice. Then it glares straight up at you.

Its clusters of eyes seem full of evil. Your heart hammers in terror.

"Grab it!" Rachel cries wildly.

Don't let that thing get away! Hurry to PAGE 119.

"Where am I?" you mumble as you open your eyes in a strange, stark-white room. Your head aches. Your mouth tastes like the inside of a garbage pail. You feel weak all over.

"You're safe in my laboratory," a man answers. His eyes gleam at you through wire-framed glasses. His silvery beard is almost as bright as his sparkling white coat.

"I'm Dr. Bronstein," he says with a phony-looking smile. "I know what happened to you — and I can help. But you must cooperate with me. I need to take some of your blood."

Blood? Do you really want to let this guy take your blood?

If you let Dr. Bronstein take your blood, turn to PAGE 65.

If you try to escape, turn to PAGE 40.

10

You start walking. Walking through one website after another. Trying to find the GOOSE-BUMPS home page.

The only problem is: You don't know how to use the virtual Internet. You left Rachel behind, so you have no guide.

Do you have any idea how vast the Internet is?

Thousands and thousands of websites. Tens of thousands of files. Millions of bits of information.

Trying to find the GOOSEBUMPS website without a guide, without the address, without a search engine . . .

It's hopeless.

On the other hand, if you close this book and open it again — to any random page — you have *some* chance of reaching a happy ending.

Maybe you'd better try that.

Because right now, you're lost in cyberspace. And when you're lost in space, you never, ever come to . . .

THE END.

Congratulations! Your memory isn't total mush yet.

You remembered the name on the letter — Digit Wizard. It has a total of eleven letters, so you turned to PAGE 11.

Which means you can also remember the way back to Rachel.

For now.

So what are you waiting for? Get going!

Hurry up — run back to Coffin City on PAGE 46.

You decide to go find Rachel.

Good plan.

The only problem is . . . your memory isn't what it used to be!

Can you remember the way back?

That depends.

Can you remember the name of the person who signed the letter in your mailbox? (Hint: It wasn't a regular name. It was a nickname or screen name.)

Count the total number of letters in the person's name. Turn to that page.

If you remember the name, turn to the page number that is the same as the total number of letters in the name.

If you don't remember, turn to PAGE 103.

Rachel leads you through a dizzying patchwork of websites. In a few moments you're at the GOOSEBUMPS site.

"Do you see anything about GOOD LUCK?" you ask her.

"Yeah — right here," Rachel replies.

You read the message that floats in the air in front of you. It says:

GOOD LUCK CODE

Rachel makes the code sound easy. It's based on the idea that three is a lucky number. So, to write secret messages in code, you just insert an extra letter for every third letter in the message.

Example: If the message is HAVE A SCARY DAY

You could write: HAPVERASICAURYKDAEY

(Every third letter is an extra one that doesn't belong!)

To decode a message: Cross out every third letter, like this:

HA~~P~~VE~~R~~AS~~I~~CA~~U~~RY~~K~~DA~~E~~Y

Now rewrite the message, leaving out all the letters that you crossed out. It will look like this:

HAVEASCARYDAY!

Turn to PAGE 101.

"I can't ignore that message," you declare. "We've got to help the web crawler."

"Fine," Mark says. "But how?"

Good question.

You stare at the screen. Suddenly another message box pops up. It covers the first message, filling the screen.

WHAT ARE YOU WAITING FOR? HELP ME **NOW**!!!

Under the message it says: CLICK HERE TO CONTINUE.

"Wait!" Mark yells.

Too late. You already clicked the mouse.

Turn quickly to PAGE 52.

You stare down at a wormy, bony arm.

It's a corpse, all right. And it's trying to pull you into a grave!

Thinking fast, you drop down and roll, twisting the bones. The corpse lets go — just long enough for you to jump up and leap away.

You're safe!

"Got you now!" a horrible voice snarls behind you.

You whirl. Crusher!

"Now it's my turn," he says. "And I'm not some weak, bony skeleton. I'm going to get you good!"

You're curious. But you figure now is not the time to ask *why* Crusher wants to hurt you. Now is the time to take off.

That's what you do. You run as fast as you can. Rachel is up ahead. She's made it nearly to the edge of the cemetery.

But Crusher is closing in on you.

You pour on the speed. Soon you've caught up with Rachel.

Run to PAGE 82.

16

Back to Dr. Bronstein's office. That's the best place to go, you decide.

Good plan.

There's only one problem: Can you find the way?

You can, if you have a good sense of direction. Do you?

Find out on PAGE 34.

You decide to turn around and run back to your E-mail.

Away from the graves and the corpses and the evil Crusher.

You turn and start running back the way you came.

"No! Wait! We can't get separated!" Rachel calls after you. "It's too dangerous!"

Huh? What does she mean, *dangerous*?

"Come back!" Rachel yells. "Or you'll never get out of the Net alive!"

Well?

To go back to Rachel, turn to PAGE 6.

To keep running toward your E-mail, turn to PAGE 39.

18

You're thinking it's not the flu. It's a virus. And you know just what you got it from.

Beads of sweat form on your face and forehead.

"Man, you look sick," Mark comments. "We've got to get you to your doctor."

"My doctor. . . ?" A feeling of dread spreads in the pit of your stomach.

"I don't remember my doctor's name," you confess.

Mark seems really worried. "Wait! I know a doctor we could go to," he announces. "Or else . . ."

"Or else what?" you ask.

From the gleam in Mark's eyes, you can tell he's got some crazy plan.

Find out Mark's plan on PAGE 30.

"Sorry I split like that," Mark apologizes as he bursts into your room. "You know I don't usually get scared."

"No problemo," you reply. "But maybe we should take the computer to a computer store. I mean, we shouldn't mess with a virus. Let someone else fix it. You know?"

"A virus is nothing," Mark argues. "We can fix it ourselves. Let's plug it in and give it another try."

You hesitate, remembering the beeping noise.

"If it starts beeping, we can just pull the plug again," Mark says, as if reading your mind.

Well?

To plug in your computer again and reboot, turn to PAGE 43.

To take it to the computer store to be fixed, turn to PAGE 89.

"My older sister is parked over here," Mark says, leading you to a dark green minivan. "I made her drive me around to look for you. Now I owe her big time."

"Uh, thanks," you mumble.

"Are you okay?" Mark asks. "Why did you run out of Dr. Bronstein's office? Where have you been all day?"

"I don't know." You shrug, feeling stupid and confused.

It's weird not to know the answers to any of his questions.

All you know is that you're sick and hungry.

Your stomach growls so loud that Mark hears it.

"You hungry?" he asks as he opens the minivan door.

You nod.

"Don't worry — I've got candy in here," he says. "Get in."

Now your heart *really* starts pounding.

Candy? Are you really about to climb into a car with a stranger who's offering you *candy*?

You may not remember much, but you do know one thing: Getting into strangers' cars is totally against the rules.

The question is: Is this kid a stranger? Or your best friend?

To accept Mark's help and get in the car, turn to PAGE 85.

To turn him down and stay out of the car, turn to PAGE 104.

You knock twice. Almost immediately, the door swings open.

"Yes?" A sweet-faced woman stares at you, as if she expects you to sell her wrapping paper or cookies or something.

"Um, I'm lost," you say. "And I don't feel well. I think I'm really sick."

"You poor thing!" the woman exclaims. She swings the door open wide. "Come in, sweetheart. We'll call your parents. What's your name?"

Uh-oh! Your name? You have no idea what your name is!

You want to tell her the truth — because you always tell the truth. But how can you say that a monster jumped out of your computer and bit you, and now you have no memory?

Who would believe you?

Maybe you should make up some kind of story.

To tell her the truth, turn to PAGE 28.
To make up a story, turn to PAGE 67.

"Rachel hangs out at the Dot Com Diner," Mark says. "That's where we're going."

The Dot Com Diner is a really cool diner in town. It has couches, tables, and computers all over the place.

When you and Mark get there the place is hopping. The customers are drinking milk shakes, surfing the Internet, and chatting.

"That's her — Rachel Bronstein," Mark says.

He points to a tall girl with long red hair. She is standing in the back corner arguing with a couple of nerdy-looking guys.

"Let's hurry," you moan. "I feel really dizzy. . . ."

The room swims in front of your eyes. Everything goes blurry.

You collapse, crumpling into a big overstuffed chair.

Turn to PAGE 135.

"Plordik!" Rachel yells.

A door suddenly appears in the glass side of the building.

Whoa!

"That's the password," Rachel explains. "We're safe now."

"Safe where?" you demand. "Where are we?" You gaze around the huge room. It's filled with computer stations. A bunch of kids work keyboards and mouses, staring at their monitors.

"It's a hacker's forum," Rachel explains. "A bunch of my friends hang out here. One of them made the antidote program I was telling you about. It's supposed to cure any virus. I think he's our best shot at fixing you up."

"Great," you say. "Though I feel pretty good right now."

Rachel studies you. "You *do* look better. Hey, maybe it was all that running! Maybe all you need is a little exercise. Do you like to surf?"

Totally! You love shooting the curls!

Just thinking about it makes you feel even better.

Maybe you should go have some fun. . . .

Then again, maybe you should stick to the plan.

To search for Rachel's friend, turn to PAGE 111.

To surf the Net, turn to PAGE 74.

24

But the mouse is frozen. No matter how much you move it around or how many times you click the button, nothing happens.

The spider face starts to change shape. The colors swirl around again.

"Maybe it's going away," you mumble hopefully.

But it doesn't go away. It just changes from the shape of a four-eyed monster *head* to an *entire monster*, tentacles and all.

But that's not the worst part.

See what's worse on PAGE 78.

"No way," you whisper, shaking your head hard at Mark. "Don't listen to it."

You lean against the kitchen counter. You put your hand to your forehead. Gross! It's slick with sweat.

"I'm sweaty," you say in surprise. "And my head is throbbing like crazy." You swallow hard. "I think I'm getting sick."

Mark frowns. "No way, man," he mumbles. "You can't get a virus from a computer. Computer viruses aren't germs or anything. They're just bad programs."

"I don't care what you think," you tell him. "I'm definitely going to throw up!" You cover your mouth and make a mad dash for the bathroom.

Race to PAGE 83.

"Look at that bite!" Mark exclaims. An expression of horror fills his face.

You hurry into your room and glance in the mirror.

The bite mark is purplish-red and already swollen. It throbs.

"Is . . . is the monster gone?" you ask. Your voice trembles. You feel really sick. You begin to shake all over.

"Yeah," Mark answers. "But I have to tell you — I think we should go after it."

"Are you crazy?" you say. "I need to call my mom! She'll come home and help me."

"But by then it will be too late!" Mark insists. "We have to catch it. They'll need to test it for diseases and stuff. It has a virus, remember?"

Make up your mind!

You could call your mom . . . but then Spydie will get away.

To chase the monster, turn to PAGE 32.
To call your mom, turn to PAGE 50.

"IT EATS BANANAS." Mark reads the decoded message again. "What's that supposed to mean?"

"'It' must mean the web crawler, Spyder," Rachel guesses.

"So if the Spyder likes bananas, we put some out as bait . . . ," Mark begins.

"And lure it back to my computer," you yell. Your eyes light up with excitement.

Mark frowns. "But where do we put the bananas?"

Rachel turns to you. "I bet the Spyder is still at your house."

"No," Mark argues. "I think it's trying to find you. I bet it's right here, in the Dot Com Diner."

You shiver at the thought.

It's up to you. Where do you set the trap?

To put the banana trap at home, turn to PAGE 114.

To set the trap in the Dot Com Diner, turn to PAGE 4.

You follow the woman into a comfortable living room.

"Uh, well, see, I can't exactly remember my name," you begin.

The woman stiffens. "Why not?" she asks, giving you a cold stare.

"Uh, well, this is going to sound weird," you go on. "But there was this ... this ... thing. This monster. It crawled out of my computer. I know it sounds crazy. But it *bit* me. And ever since then, I've had some kind of weird virus. I can't remember my name, my address ... nothing."

You hold your breath, wondering what she'll say.

Find out on PAGE 77.

Your heart is racing. Sweat pours down your back.

Coming back here was a big mistake, you realize. You have to escape!

Before you can force yourself to move, the door opens. Dr. Bronstein strides in, carrying a tray.

"Sit up, sit up, my friend," he says. "I brought you dinner."

Yes!

You swing your legs over the edge of the table. Then you catch a glimpse of dinner.

Find out what's on your plate on PAGE 97.

"There's this doctor my dad knows," Mark begins. "Dr. Bronstein. You could go to him. Or . . ."

"Or *what?*" you demand. "Come on. Just say it!"

"Or you could ask his daughter Rachel for help," Mark suggests. "She's, like, a teenager or something."

"His daughter?" you mumble. You wipe a sweaty palm across your forehead. "Why would I ask a kid for help?"

"She's a total computer whiz," Mark explains. "She can hack into anything. She changed my sister's grades to all F's. Just for the fun of it."

You moan. "But I'm sick! I need a *real* doctor!"

"But what if you don't have a real flu?" Mark says. "What if you have a *computer* virus?"

What do you want to do?

To get medical help, visit Dr. Bronstein on PAGE 75.

To visit a computer expert, find Rachel Bronstein on PAGE 22.

The mailbox. The grassy road.

They're still there!

You glance down at the visor and headset in your hands. You've taken them off, but . . .

You haven't returned to the real world.

You're still in the Internet.

Trapped there. Forever!

And guess who is right there waiting for you?

That's right — Crusher, the evil, tattooed kid with the swinging chain.

Well, maybe you two can become friends.

You can form your own chain gang!

THE END

"You're right," you tell Mark. "We've got to find that Spyder thing. If it has some disease, we've got to know!"

"Come on!" Mark shouts. "It went down the stairs!"

You both hurtle down the stairs that lead to the kitchen.

You stare at the kitchen table and chairs, the cabinets and countertops.

"It could be anywhere," you say.

You glance at Mark. He looks as terrified as you feel.

"Unless . . . ," Mark begins. His eyes go wide.

"Unless what?" you ask.

You won't find out unless you turn to PAGE 100.

Then you hear a sharp *CLICK*!

As if by magic, the door suddenly swings open.

Standing in front of you is a teenage girl with long red hair. Freckles are sprinkled all over her face.

"I brought you some coffee, Dad," she says. When she sees you she looks totally confused.

"Rachel!" Dr. Bronstein cries. "Bad timing! Close that door!"

"Too late!" you yell. "I'm out of here!"

You push past Rachel and race into the cold, white hallway. To a stairway. Down six flights of steps.

Dr. Bronstein chases after you. But you're younger. Faster.

At the bottom of the steps, you burst through a large metal door. You're free!

Run to PAGE 59.

Ever since you left Dr. Bronstein's office, you've been wandering, turning right and then left. Then left. Then right.

You've made so many twists and taken so many turns, you feel like a pretzel!

The big question is: Can you remember enough to find your way through the dark streets to his office?

Sure, you think.

And to prove it, you fill in the maze on page 35 — using a pen, not a pencil!

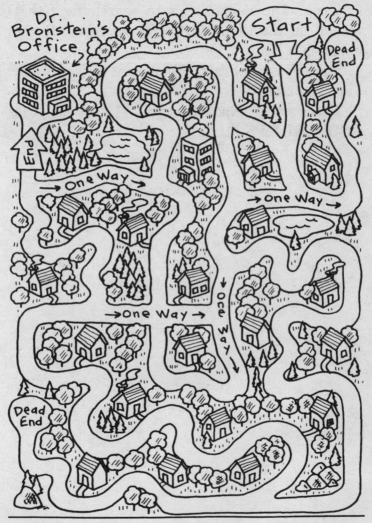

If you got through the maze without making any mistakes, congratulations! Your great sense of direction will help you turn to PAGE 63.

If you didn't make it through, you'd better turn to PAGE 54.

"Look. The E-mail says to search for GOOD LUCK on the GOOSEBUMPS website," Rachel explains.

"Right," you murmur. Your head feels so foggy. You can't think!

"Come on," Rachel says. "Let's hit that GOOSEBUMPS site."

Turn to PAGE 13.

"That's your web crawler," Mark says.

You grin.

"The monster is 'Spyder.' Cool!" You punch in a few commands. "So let's delete Spyder," you say as you're typing. "That should delete the virus, right?"

"Right, and it will also get rid of whatever is sending you those weird messages," Mark agrees.

But before you finish typing, a new message pops up on your computer screen.

DON'T TRY TO DELETE ME!

"Whoa!" you cry. "Whoever wrote this program is *good*."

"They guessed you'd try to delete it!" Mark exclaims. "Try the mouse."

Turn to PAGE 24.

Wow!

You jump onto the surfboard. Within seconds, you're zooming over waves of computer information. On crests of websites. And over a sea of programs and databases and files.

It's weird. In your mind, you know this is only a visual trick. You're *really* standing in the Peach Pit.

But you don't care about what's real. You love it! The images are so real — you totally forget about being sick.

You cut sideways to catch a wave to another website.

"Okay — fun's over!" Rachel calls. "Let's get going."

"In a minute," you call back to her. "I just want to catch this next wave!"

Ride the wave to PAGE 116.

Who cares what Rachel says? you think. You just want to get away from that guy with the tattoos. And Coffin City.

Besides — you're feeling weaker every minute. Sicker.

The virus is taking over every inch of your body.

You glance over your shoulder.

Crusher is right on your tail!

"You're mine!" he yells, swinging the heavy chain.

Why is he after me? you wonder. What did I do to him?

But you don't have the breath to ask.

Maybe you should just rip off the headset and visor. Put an end to this virtual Internet thing.

That way, you'd be right back in Rachel's Peach Pit. Right?

But a few steps ahead, you spot the mailbox again.

Your mailbox.

Your E-mail is still waiting for you. . . .

If you want to read the E-mail in your mailbox, turn to PAGE 105.

If you take off the virtual reality gear, turn to PAGE 118.

No way, you think. No way am I going to let this freaky doctor take my blood!

You've got to escape. Get out of this crazy laboratory. But how?

You glance quickly around the room.

Across from you is a door. It's closed. You can't tell whether it's locked.

Nearer to you, you see a window. An open window.

But who knows how high up you are? If you jump out of a top floor window, you might break your leg — or worse.

Dr. Bronstein sees you checking out the escape routes.

"Oh, no, you don't," he says, coming at you with an evil gleam in his eye.

Hurry up. Pick one!

To jump out the window, turn to PAGE 48.
To race for the door, turn to PAGE 95.

"Cool!" Mark exclaims, gazing at the wild room.

The walls of the Peach Pit are painted in shades of — you guessed it — peach. A swirling mass in shades of pink and orange. The colors spiral around and around on the walls.

"Kind of psychedelic, isn't it?" Rachel asks you and Mark.

"Yeah," you answer weakly. You don't tell her it makes you even more sick to your stomach.

Instead you head straight for the huge computer monitor. It's the size of a giant-screen TV. Below it, on a high-tech metal desk, is the computer itself. And a keyboard.

More cool stuff is dangling from the ceiling. Joysticks. Headsets. Goggles. Visors. All the stuff for virtual reality games. They're bouncing and dangling on colorful elastic cords.

Rachel points at Mark, then at a chair. "You — sit," she orders. "So you won't be in our way."

Then she grabs a set of hand controls and a visor and tosses them to you. "You — stand beside me. We're going on-line. Into the virtual Internet. Put on your gear!"

Enter the virtual Internet on PAGE 57.

"Use the scanner!" you shout.

Rachel lets go of the Spyder and slips the scanner out of her backpack. It looks like a miniature copy machine.

"I'll set it up and turn on the computer," Rachel says.

"Hurry!" you shout.

The squirming monster starts to hiss. It thrashes even harder in your hands.

Rachel opens the lid of the scanner. "Now!" she shouts.

You and Mark press the Spyder onto the glass.

"Press the button! Scan it in!" you scream.

Rachel presses a button.

BZZZZZZ...

Lights flash. A moment later, an image of the monster, Spyder, appears on your monitor screen.

"Help!" you cry, trying to hold on to the Spyder. "It's getting away!"

Turn to PAGE 127.

"All right, Mark. I'm game," you declare. "Let's reboot and give it another shot!"

You boot up your computer again.

Everything seems normal.

You log on to the Internet. Instead of a message, a weird, swirling image appears.

"What *is* that?" Mark asks.

"I don't know," you answer as a face starts to form. The face of a hideous monster.

Two sharp pincers snap open and closed.

Yellow pus squirts out of its mouth.

"Wait a minute!" Mark shouts. "What was the name of that web crawler you got?"

"Spyder," you answer.

Then that means . . .

What does it mean? Turn to PAGE 37.

You decide to stick with Rachel. She's the computer whiz. Without her, you're lost.

You and Rachel take the elevator to the eighteenth floor.

"There he is!" Rachel points to a kid with the long beard and pointed hat of a wizard.

"A wizard?" you wonder aloud.

"Well, his real name is Dave Wiener," Rachel explains. "But that's so wimpy — he just goes by his screen name."

"Hi, I'm Digit Wizard," the kid says.

Digit Wizard? Hmmm . . . Haven't you heard that name before?

If you have, turn to PAGE 53.
If you haven't, turn to PAGE 5.

Your head is throbbing with headache and fever. Your arms and legs hurt each time you move. You're sweating and you're weak from hunger. But inside Dr. Bronstein's office, you begin to relax.

At least it's warm in here, you think. And maybe he's got food around.

"Can I have something to eat?" you whisper.

"Not yet," Dr. Bronstein says. "Not until I've tested your blood."

Uh-oh. You forgot about that part.

You hate needles. But you'd do anything for food.

"Okay," you answer, sticking out your arm. "Just do it!"

You close your eyes and turn your head away.

Dr. Bronstein fills a vial with your blood. "This is good. Very good," he says. "I'll be right back."

Then he rushes out of the room — locking the door behind him.

You're locked in!

Try not to panic till you reach PAGE 29.

46

You race along the road, back to the graveyard. You're starting to feel pretty weak. But you have to keep going.

Finally, the graveyard is in sight.

You stop dead in your tracks. Rachel is in the middle of a karate fight with a skeleton! The two of them are battling at the edge of an empty grave.

"Umph!" Rachel grunts as the skeleton flips her from behind.

Rachel stumbles backward, falling into the open grave.

Yuck!

The skeleton runs away, cackling.

"Help!" Rachel screams. "Somebody help me!"

Oh, man. You hope you have enough strength to haul her out of there. Sweating, you throw yourself down on the ground and reach over the edge of the grave.

Reaching to give Rachel a hand.

But another arm shoots out of the grave.

A tattooed arm. And it reaches for your throat!

Matters get even graver *on PAGE 64.*

"I guess we'd better let it out," you tell Mark.

"*I'm* not opening that door," Mark says, backing up. "That thing *bit* me!"

"It bit *me* too," you snap. "But we're both going to get sick, and I want to know what the cure is. Didn't you hear what it said?"

Mark won't budge. So finally you reach for the cabinet door handle. You quickly swing it open, then jerk your arm back, out of the way.

You don't want *another* bite.

RATTLE! BANG!

Bottles and cans fall over as Spydie pokes its hideous head into the kitchen.

Your heart is pounding. But you try to act fearless.

"Are you coming out or not?" you demand.

Find out on PAGE 70.

You go for the window.

Your heart pounds as you leap off the examining table and make a dash for it.

Don't think, you tell yourself. Just jump!

"Ahhhhhh!" you scream as you throw yourself through the open window. You begin to fall through tree limbs, bashing against them as you hurtle toward the ground.

Jump out a window?

You must have been sicker than you thought, to make a choice like that!

A leap of faith is one thing. . . .

But this is more like a leap to

THE END!

A voice calls your name.

Who is it? The computer? But you killed it with the spray!

You spin around.

It's not the computer.

It's worse than that.

"M-M-Mom," you stutter, trying to smile. "Aren't you supposed to be at work?"

Your mom stands in your doorway. Staring at your ruined computer. She does *not* look happy.

"What are you doing?" she demands. "That was a brand-new computer. Do you know how much it cost your father and me?"

"I, uh . . . it had a bug. A virus. And . . ." You babble on about the error messages. And the horrible beeping. And how the computer told you to use bug spray.

But it's no use. Your computer is toast, your room stinks of bug spray — and your mom is furious.

"I can't believe this!" She shakes her head as if to clear it. "Stay in your room until I decide on your punishment."

Learn your fate on PAGE 61.

"I'm sick," you moan. "Call my mom at work. She'll know what to do."

"Fine," Mark says. "What's her phone number?"

"I don't know," you reply. "I can't remember."

Mark stares at you as if you're nuts. "You can't remember your mom's phone number?" He takes a breath. "Okay — I'll look it up. Where does she work?"

"I can't remember," you say.

"Are you kidding?" Mark asks.

You shake your head. "I ... I can't remember anything," you stammer. "My face is hot. My throat is sore. My stomach hurts like crazy. And I think I'm going to throw up."

"Okay, don't panic," Mark says. "You're probably getting the flu."

"The flu?" you say uncertainly. "Yeah — maybe."

But from the expression on Mark's face, you know what he's thinking. The same thing *you're* thinking.

Think you can make it to PAGE 18?

The cabinet door flies open. The hideous blue monster leaps out.

It plants itself in the middle of the kitchen floor.

"Ha-ha — tricked you," it sneers. Yellow pus drips from its mouth. "There *is* no cure for the virus!"

Spydie laughs and laughs.

You glance around for a weapon. You grab the first thing you find — a yellow plastic spatula. It's not much. But it's better than nothing.

"Stay away from me," you warn the monster. "Or I'll —"

"You won't do anything," Spydie interrupts. "You can't. The virus is erasing your memory too fast. You probably don't even remember what that plastic thing is."

Uh-oh. It's true. You stare at the yellow thing in your hand. You have no idea what it does.

But you can't let Spydie know it's right. So you bluff.

"I do too know what this is for!" you declare. "It's for . . ."

If you think it's for flipping pancakes, turn to PAGE 125.

If you think it's for swatting flies, turn to PAGE 92.

Another message pops up on the screen.

You and Mark read it and begin to chuckle. You start laughing first, then Mark. Soon you're both doubled over, screaming with laughter.

THIS BUG IS KILLING ME! GET A CAN OF BUG SPRAY, WILL YOU?

OPEN UP YOUR COMPUTER AND SPRAY YOUR HARD DRIVE.

"Bug spray?" Mark sputters. "Man, oh, man!"

"Somebody's got a sense of humor," you mutter, wiping tears from your eyes.

But your computer starts to beep again. This time it's even longer, louder, and more earsplitting than before.

And this time, it doesn't stop.

You clamp your hands over your ears.

BEEEEEEEEP!

It's so loud, you feel as if your eardrums are going to burst.

"Ow!" Mark screams, covering his ears and bolting out of your room. "I'm out of here!"

"But what should I do?" you yell after him.

Mark doesn't answer.

Follow Mark to PAGE 69.

"Digit Wizard?" you repeat. You know that name!

"Yeah. You got my letter, huh?" Digit Wizard replies.

Your head starts spinning in confusion. The letter?

Then you remember. The E-mail!

"You? You sent that letter?" you cry. "Then you're the one who gave me the virus!"

"What letter?" Rachel demands.

Quickly you show her the E-mail. Rachel looks shocked.

"I don't believe you, Digit!" she cries.

He smiles wickedly. "I have to get my kicks somehow."

Before you can reply, he saunters away.

You think hard. The letter must have some kind of clue to finding the antidote!

"Could it be the number of words in the E-mail?" you mumble.

"No way. It's the website," Rachel tells you. "The answer we need must be on the GOOSE-BUMPS website. Like it says in the E-mail."

Which is it?

If you think the clue is on the GOOSEBUMPS website, turn to PAGE 36.

If you think the clue is the number of words in the E-mail letter, turn to PAGE 120.

54

You realize you're too sick and tired to move. You'd never find your way back to the lab to see that doctor.

What was his name again?

You drop to your knees and curl up in a ball on the ground.

Ouch, you think. The ground is hard. And cold.

You close your eyes to block out the glare from the streetlights overhead.

"Hey," a kid's voice says, startling you.

You open your eyes and see a huge figure looming over you.

Your heart pounds with fear.

The kid looks really tough.

"What are you doing here?" he demands.

He sounds tough too.

"Answer me!" he shouts.

Better answer on PAGE 81.

You gaze at the boy standing beside you.

Wait a minute. He isn't a boy.

He's a Spyder. Like you!

With eight tentacles for legs, it's easy to crawl onto the desk. You gaze at the computer screen. You lift one tentacle. You punch it at the screen. It slides through easily.

You lift another tentacle. Then another. Then three more.

You push, and your whole body falls into the computer.

You're completely inside now!

As you crawl toward the other Spyders, you dimly realize that your life as a human has reached

THE END.

You and Mark stare in horror at the enormous creature on your desk.

It's about the size of a small cat.

Its four huge eyes look as if they belong on a tarantula.

Its big, squishy body looks as if it belongs on an octopus.

"What's wrong with you?" the monster, Spyder, snarls. "I asked you to help me. But you didn't." It stamps one of its hairy tentacles.

You and Mark back up a few more feet. Slowly.

"Now Spydie is very, very angry with you," the monster growls.

"Spydie?" You and Mark exchange a glance.

"Let's make a break for the door," Mark whispers.

"Okay," you whisper back. "But we better move fast."

You both leap toward the bedroom door. You grab the doorknob. You're about to wrench open the door when you hear a terrifying scream behind you.

You duck instinctively. Spydie flies past your shoulder — and smacks against the door, slamming it shut.

Then the monster faces you.

"Going somewhere?" it asks.

Answer on PAGE 108.

"What's the virtual Internet?" you ask.

"It's just the regular Internet," Rachel explains. "But with this equipment of mine, it feels like you're actually walking — or surfing — the websites. See?"

Wow! When you put on the equipment, you *do* see. It looks and feels as if you've actually stepped into a different world!

Colored paths and signs surround you. You feel as if you're standing on a giant quilt. Except the quilt is made of websites!

It kind of takes your mind off being sick.

"All I have to do is point to something," Rachel says, "and we go there. But we can get there faster if we walk."

"Walk?" you repeat.

"Yeah, walk. You know — move your feet," Rachel says impatiently.

See if you can remember how to walk on PAGE 68.

Wait a minute!

This can't be real, you tell yourself.

It's just a kid wearing a black gorilla suit.

A *big* kid wearing a gorilla suit.

The kid lunges at you and grabs the bananas from your hands.

"Cut it out!" you yell. "I need those!" You leap at him and try to wrestle the fruit away.

"Are you crazy?" Mark says. "Let him have the stupid bananas!"

"He's just a kid in a gorilla suit," you insist.

"That's no kid!" Rachel yells. "Give him the bananas!"

You gulp and thrust the bananas at the gorilla.

Too late. He doesn't want them anymore.

He wants *you*.

He wraps you in his huge arms and squeezes. Hard.

As you start to pass out, you realize you should have remembered the old joke:

Q: What does a three-hundred-pound gorilla eat for breakfast?

A: Anything he wants!

THE END

You race down the street and around the corner without stopping.

Finally, a few blocks away, panting and out of breath, you collapse. You drop to the ground on a lush lawn in front of a big yellow house that has roses by its front door.

The coast is clear. The doctor has lost your trail.

Come to think of it, he's not the only one who's lost!

You don't recognize the street. Or the neighborhood. You have no idea where you are. Or where you want to go.

In fact, you can't remember a thing!

What are you doing here, anyway?

A terrible fear jolts through your body. You feel so alone. You want to just curl up under the bushes and hide.

But you can't just hide. You're sick — and you're starting to get hungry.

You need help. You could knock on the door of the yellow house. Or you could start walking and hope you recognize someone or something.

Which will it be?

If you decide to start walking, turn to PAGE 117.

If you knock on the door of the yellow house, turn to PAGE 128.

Calm down, you tell yourself. You're in your own house. You grew up here. Of *course* you know where the bathroom is.

But you don't.

Your memory is already being erased. That's what this computer virus does.

Luckily, you spot a glimpse of white tile through an open door. You make it into the bathroom just in time.

When you're done being sick, you stumble back down the hall. Somehow, you find your way back to the kitchen.

"Uh-oh," Mark tells you. "I think I'm going to be sick too!" He lurches forward, covering his mouth with both hands.

"Nooooo!" you cry. "Don't let go of that cabinet door!"

Too late.

Go to PAGE 51.

Your mom slams your bedroom door. *Really* slams it. With an incredibly loud *BANG!*

"Ow!" you hear her say.

But you don't dare poke your head outside to see if she's okay. After all, she told you to stay in your room. And that's exactly what you're going to do!

Too bad you don't know that your mom just hit herself on the head with the door. Now she's got amnesia!

She doesn't remember anything — her name, her address, nothing! She doesn't even remember that she has a kid.

And she certainly doesn't remember telling you to stay in your room.

Looks like you'll be here for a very long time. Too bad your computer is fried. At least you could have played some video games to pass the time.

Now you'll be staring at that blank screen until

THE END.

The cruel words leap off the page at you.

From the way your whole body is shaking with chills, you know the letter tells the truth. You *are* going to die — unless you do something soon!

But what?

You remember what Rachel said a moment ago. That you would never get out of the Internet alive — unless you and she stayed together.

Maybe you should turn back and try to find Rachel.

You shiver at the thought of going through Coffin City again. Maybe you should search for the GOOSEBUMPS website instead. Like it said in the letter. Go to the GOOSEBUMPS website and look for GOOD LUCK there.

Your head pounds. Your stomach heaves. The fever makes you feel as if you're burning up one minute and freezing the next.

You'd better hurry. . . .

If you go back to find Rachel, turn to PAGE 12.
If you search for the GOOSEBUMPS website, turn to PAGE 10.

Your sense of direction is so good, your friends call you the Human Compass.

You have no trouble finding your way back to Dr. Bronstein's office. You arrive just as he's leaving.

"Ah, my little friend!" He grabs you in a big hug. "You came back to me!"

"Y-y-yes," you stutter, shivering from the cold night air. "I'm s-s-s-sick. Can you help me?"

"I can . . . and I will. *If* you'll do what I tell you." Dr. Bronstein gives you a questioning stare over the top of his round glasses.

"Sure," you answer. "Okay. I'll d-d-do whatever you say."

"Good," Dr. Bronstein says, grinning and rubbing his hands together. "Come with me."

Follow Dr. Bronstein into his office on PAGE 45.

Crusher, the tattooed guy, is in the grave with Rachel. And he has you by the neck!

With a powerful jerk, Crusher tries to pull you down, into the dark, moist pit.

"Aaahhhh!" you scream as you fight back with all your strength.

You can't let Crusher get you. You can't.

A weird tingling sensation runs through your body. For a split second, you feel as if you're going to be sick. But that's not what's happening.

What's happening is . . . no!

It's too creepy for words. It can't be.

Or can it?

Find out on PAGE 124.

Right now, Dr. Bronstein seems like your best chance to get well.

"All right, go ahead. Take my blood," you agree.

"Good! Good!" Dr. Bronstein actually rubs his hands together, like an evil scientist on TV.

Your blood runs cold. But what choice do you have?

You try not to moan as the needle pierces your skin.

"Very nice, very nice," the doctor murmurs as dark red blood fills a couple of test tubes. "I'm going to make a lot of money!"

Money?

Just what kind of plans does this doctor have for you?

Find out on PAGE 102.

For a moment, you stare at one another in disbelief. Then Mark cheers.

"You did it!" He slaps Rachel a high five.

"*We* did it," Rachel corrects him.

"Hey, guess what?" You blink in surprise. "I don't feel sick anymore! My headache and chills are gone!"

Mark narrows his eyes. "Is your memory back? What's your mother's name?"

"Valerie," you reply, grinning. "I even know *your* mom's name! It's Anne!" You throw your head back and laugh.

"I'm out of here," Rachel says, heading for the door. "Come on, you guys. Let's go celebrate!"

But before she can turn the knob, you all hear a strange beep. Coming from your computer.

Uh-oh!

Turn to PAGE 72.

"What's my name?" you repeat.

You can't tell this pleasant-looking lady the truth. That you don't remember.

"Uh, it's a secret," you say. "My, uh, my parents work for a secret government agency. And I help them. We go around to yellow houses to taste the food. So, if you could lead me to the kitchen, I could taste yours. And then maybe I could test out your beds. Just for a little nap . . ."

The woman raises her eyebrows.

"A secret government agency?" she repeats. "I see. Just wait here a minute, dear. I'll be right back."

She quickly slips into the kitchen. You can hear her dialing the phone.

Uh-oh.

Trace that call to PAGE 80.

"It's easy," you hear Rachel's voice say. "Just walk in place."

Okay, you think, as you start to move your feet, one in front of the other.

As soon as you start moving, the view in your visor changes. It's as if you are walking *through* the websites!

"This is so cool!" you exclaim.

You and Rachel begin walking through the grassy green countryside.

You pass a mailbox standing by the side of the road. You see a letter inside — addressed to you. It's your E-mail, you realize.

"Hey, look!" you call to Rachel. "I've got mail!"

You crane your neck as you bend over and reach into the mailbox.

"Watch out!" Rachel warns. "There's a man . . ."

Too late — a heavy hand falls on your shoulder. You jump and whirl around.

It's a man wearing an old-fashioned black cloak with a hood.

The hood falls back. You gasp. His face is horrible.

It's a white mass of rotting flesh!

Scream your guts out on PAGE 73.

Mark races downstairs. In a flash, he's out your back door.

You're right behind him. But you stop in the kitchen and gulp down a few deep breaths.

The beep is so loud it rattles the dishes in the sink.

You have to stop that stupid noise!

Should you pull the plug on the whole computer? *That* should make the beeping stop.

Or should you do what the message says? Grab some bug spray and fumigate your hard drive?

One thing's for sure — you've got to act fast. Before your teeth split apart from that awful beeping!

If you reach for the bug spray, turn to PAGE 84.
If you turn off the computer, turn to PAGE 99.

"You made the right decision to let me out of there!" Spydie tells you.

"Ugh, gross," Mark mutters, as the monster's mouth drips yellow pus onto the floor.

"Just tell us the cure," you demand. "I feel sick already. I'm all hot and sweaty — and shaky too."

"That's the virus, all right," Spydie says. "It's erasing your memory. Pretty soon you won't remember the rules of your favorite sports. You won't remember your best friend's name. You won't even know the words to 'Mary Had a Little Lamp.'"

"Little *Lamp*? That's not right." Mark frowns. "Or is it?"

You shrug. "It sounds right to me."

"You're forgetting things already," the monster points out.

"Okay, okay," you say. "We let you out. Now keep your word. How do we get better?"

"Yeah," Mark adds. "What's the cure for this thing?"

Spydie chuckles. A deep, mean-sounding chuckle.

Find out why it's laughing on PAGE 133.

Rachel points to the P.S. "There's your coded message!" she exclaims. "We've got to cross out every third letter." She quickly writes the P.S. on a clean sheet of paper.

It says: ITOEARTSEBAQNAPNAIS

Starting with the letter I, cross out every third letter.

Then rewrite the message here — without the crossed-out letters.

——————————————————

The words in the new message will all run together. Figure out where to separate them to read the message.

After you decode the message, turn to PAGE 27.

You march over to the monitor.

A message has popped up on your screen. It says:

THIS IS YOUR HARD DRIVE. I KNOW HOW YOU CAN WIN THE LOTTERY. DO WHAT I SAY — AND YOU WILL MAKE TEN MILLION DOLLARS!

"Now that's the kind of computer message I like!" you say.

"Me too," Mark agrees.

"Me three!" Rachel adds.

You rush over to your desk and log on. Hey, the three of you beat a deadly virus and destroyed a monster web crawler. Compared to that, making ten million dollars has to be a total breeze. Right?

THE END

You leap back from the hideous man. Your heart pounds.

"I forgot to warn you," Rachel says. "This is Coffin City. It's only a computer game — it can't hurt you. But we have to pass through it to get where we're going. Just run!"

Your heart beats even faster as you race behind Rachel through the Coffin City game. You pass a skeleton with long blond hair. A rotting dead man with a powdery white face.

It's just a game, you tell yourself. I'm not really here.

But then, a really mean-looking teenager with tattoos on both arms swings a chain at you. You hear the *WHOOSH* as it misses your head by an inch.

"I'm going to get you, Rachel!" the kid yells. "You and your friend are dead meat!"

"Oh, no!" Rachel grabs your arm. "Let's go," she urges, sounding scared. "They don't call him Crusher for nothing. Come on. We can hide in a grave."

A grave?

Maybe you'd rather forget this whole sick adventure. Maybe you'd rather just go back and check your E-mail.

To hide in a grave with Rachel, turn to PAGE 6.
To go back and check your E-mail, turn to PAGE 17.

"Surf! Definitely," you reply. It's the best idea you've heard since you got sick.

"Okay," Rachel says. "We'll surf first. But be sure to meet me back here when I tell you. I still think we should find my friend and talk to him."

Rachel clicks her mouse. A surfboard suddenly appears, floating in front of you. Another one appears in front of Rachel.

"Hop on," she instructs. "We can really move through the Internet on these things."

Grab your board and surf over to PAGE 38.

"I feel really sick. I need a doctor," you decide. "A real doctor — not a computer nut."

"Okay," Mark says. "I'll call Dr. Bronstein's office. Stay there — and, uh, bundle up or something. You're shaking like a leaf."

You nod and curl up on your bed, pulling the covers around your shoulders. You're so cold, your teeth are chattering.

You lie back and close your eyes.

I'll just nap for a bit, you think.

When you open your eyes, some kid with big combat boots and dark wavy hair is standing beside you. He's shaking your arm to wake you up.

Your heart pounds. How come some kid you've never seen before is in your bedroom?

Find out who it is on PAGE 88.

"That Spyder-kid might know something that could help me," you tell Rachel.

"Okay," Rachel says. "I'll check out the tenth floor. I'll meet you back up here!"

You gather your courage and walk over to the table where the Spyder-kid is chatting with the the wolf-head woman.

"Hi," you say awkwardly. "I was wondering, uh —"

You're cut off by a threatening growl.

"What's the password?" the wolf-head woman growls.

"I don't know," you admit.

She bares sharp teeth.

"I — I — I'm sorry . . . ," you stammer, backing away from the table.

She lunges at you, sharp teeth snapping.

Aiming right for your throat!

Race to PAGE 87.

A weird smile comes over the woman's face. A corner of her mouth twitches.

"A monster! From a computer?" She chuckles. "And it bit you? That sounds just like a science fiction story on TV!"

"Yeah," you reply warily. "Sort of . . ."

The lady seems really excited by your story. A little too excited.

"Oh, I love science fiction stories," she gushes. "Have you seen that new TV show about space monsters? Did you see the part where the alien melts, and the human beings scoop him up, trying to help and . . ."

She goes on and on and on about some dumb TV show.

"Um, wait a minute," you try to explain. "I'm not talking about science fiction."

Still talking, she clamps a hand on your arm and pulls you toward the den.

"Look, darling!" she calls into the den. "Look what I found!"

You look in the den. And stop.

Dead in your tracks.

Make tracks to PAGE 110.

The worst part is that one of the monster's tentacles is pushing against the screen.

And the screen bulges out.

"The bump...," you murmur. "I forgot all about it."

"I don't believe it," Mark whispers.

"I told you!" you cry as the bulge gets bigger and bigger.

The screen suddenly splits. A blue tentacle bursts through and waves around in the air.

"Yikes!" you yell. You and Mark jump back from the computer.

The next minute, another tentacle pokes out. Then another. Then another.

Finally, the entire Spyder monster bursts out of your monitor. It plops onto your desk and gropes across, feeling its way across the piles of papers and pencils.

Grope your way to PAGE 56.

"Let's go find the spider-monster," you decide. "I'll never feel safe while it's walking around loose."

Rachel nods. The three of you head for the door.

You spread out, combing the neighborhood. You search the park. The school. Little shops and stores.

"Have you seen a spider-monster?" you, Rachel, and Mark ask everyone you see. "It's about the size of a cat, with eight tentacles, four eyes, and a pus-covered mouth. . . ."

Everyone interrupts you with chuckles and guffaws.

Or they stare at you as if you're stark-raving mad.

The search is so hopeless, the three of you *are* starting to go crazy!

Keep looking on PAGE 112.

Who did she call? you wonder. The police? The nearest mental hospital?

You should probably run. But you're too tired.

Anyway, the doorbell starts ringing before you can do anything. Two men burst into the kitchen and take you away.

Turns out they're actually from a secret government agency. An agency studying the effects of computer viruses.

They take you to a huge laboratory and run experiments on you. You spend every day running through mazes like a lab rat.

They're trying to find out how fast you'll learn your way through the maze and be rewarded with a piece of cheese.

But since you can't remember much, you *never* learn your way through the maze.

You don't even realize that you told the truth after all. You *are* working for a secret government agency.

In fact, if you had any brains left, you'd be happy to come to such a satisfying

END.

"What are you doing here?" the kid repeats.

"D-d-don't hurt me! I don't have any money or anything," you stammer.

"I've been looking for you all day!" the kid says. A smile breaks out on his face. "I was so worried! It's me. Mark." The kid moves sideways into the light so you can see him better.

He has wavy dark hair and he's wearing combat boots.

Mark? Who's Mark? you wonder, feeling frightened.

"It's me," he repeats. "Your best friend. Don't you remember *anything*?"

"No," you answer. "Are you really my best friend?"

The kid nods. And from the look on his face, you think he's telling the truth. At least you decide to trust him.

"Come on." Mark reaches down and pulls you to your feet. "There's somebody who wants to see you."

See who it is on PAGE 20.

Rachel grabs your arm and runs toward a huge glass office building.

"Now what?" you ask. "Where are you taking me?"

Rachel doesn't answer. She simply drags you toward the glass wall.

"Wait — there's no door!" you cry.

Are you going to crash? Find out on PAGE 23.

You race into the hallway. But when you get there, you suddenly freeze.

Which way is the bathroom?

You can't remember!

Hurry to PAGE 60 before this gets ugly.

You grab a can of bug spray from under the kitchen sink. You grab a screwdriver, then race back upstairs to your room.

BEEEEEEEEEEEEEEEP! BEEEEEEE-EEEEEEEEEEEEEEP!

Your head throbs as you unscrew the cover on your computer. You press the nozzle on the can.

SSSSSSTTT!

Clouds of white foam shoot out.

You cover the whole inside of your expensive computer with insect killer. The hard drive. The memory chips. The motherboard.

You hold your breath so you won't inhale any of the poison fumes.

You hear a bunch of crackling noises as the electronic parts sizzle. A few sparks fly, then flicker out.

Finally, the terrible beeping stops.

"Yes!" you shout, pumping your fist in the air.

But the next sound you hear sends ice through your veins.

Shiver your way to PAGE 49.

You decide to get in the car with Mark.

Normally, you'd never get into a car with a stranger — no matter what.

But this guy can't be a stranger. He knows all about you and where you've been. He knows more about you than you can remember.

"I'm glad we found you," Mark's older sister says as you climb in. "You look awful!"

"Thanks a lot!" you say sarcastically. You turn to Mark. "Where are we going?"

"To find Rachel Bronstein," Mark says.

"Rachel Bronstein?" you ask, trying not to show how confused you are. "Who's that?"

Find out on PAGE 22.

86

For the rest of the day, you watch as the monster bites every human being it can find.

Later, you hear that it's bitten everyone in your whole town. In the whole country.

Within a year, everyone in the world has been bitten.

Each person's memory has been completely erased.

There isn't a human being left on Earth who can remember his or her own name.

But they don't mind. After all, computers have taken over the world.

Computers know best.

Whoops. Looks like you should have found a better weapon than a spatula. Because right now, all you've got is a blank mind — and a lot of egg on your face.

And that means the yolk's on you.

THE END

The wolf-lady pushes you to the floor.

"You've got to know the password," she growls. "Or you get terminated!"

You feel her fangs sink into your throat.

This story is over, fangs to you!

THE END

"It's me — Mark," the kid replies.

Mark? Who's Mark?

"What are you doing here?" you ask fearfully. "Get out. Get out of my room!"

"Oh, man," the kid moans, rolling his eyes. "You're really losing it. Don't you remember *anything* anymore?"

Good question, you think. Do I remember anything?

Before you can answer, you fall back into a fitful sleep. While you toss and turn you hear voices.

"My friend is right in here, Dr. B.," a boy's voice says.

"This looks very bad," a deep voice booms. "You say a computer did this? We've got to go to my lab! Right now!"

You feel yourself being lifted like a sack of potatoes and slung over someone's shoulder.

You know you're in terrible trouble. But you're so sick, you can't even get out a peep of protest.

Feel yourself carried to PAGE 9.

"I never messed with a virus before," you tell Mark. "And I'm not going to start now. Let's get this to the store."

A week later, the store manager calls to say it's ready.

You hurry to the store. "What was wrong with it?" you ask.

"Everything!" the manager exclaims. "Viruses all over the place. New ones that I've never seen before. But don't worry — we erased them." And he hands you a bill.

You glance at it and gulp. The repairs cost hundreds of dollars! "Uh — my mom will pay for this," you say quickly.

Then you scram.

That night, you boot up, eager to try your newest game. A weird, tingling shock travels up your fingers from the keyboard.

The next morning, you're too weak to get out of bed. Your mom says you're running a really high fever. "Must be a virus," she murmurs.

Your fever goes higher . . . and higher . . . and that's the last thing you remember before

THE END!

"It came out of the monitor," you decide. "So I say we put it back in."

You, Rachel, and Mark slam the squirming Spyder against the monitor's glass screen.

"Okay, push!" you yell.

The three of you push as hard as you can.

SPLATTT!

Uh-oh. Looks like you pushed a little *too* hard.

Turn to PAGE 106.

You walk and walk. Wandering aimlessly. Past houses. Stores. A movie theater. A parking lot.

At last you've been wandering the streets for so long that it's dark out. The streetlights blink on.

You're so tired it's scary. Maybe you should just lie down in this parking lot and never get up.

But then another idea occurs to you.

Why don't you turn around? Go back to Dr. Bronstein's.

At least his office was warm. And he had food.

And maybe he wasn't such a bad guy after all. Well?

To go back to Dr. Bronstein's office, turn to PAGE 16.

To lie down on the ground, turn to PAGE 54.

"It's for . . . killing flies," you say with uncertainty.

"What are flies?" Spydie asks.

You hesitate. "Are they . . . spider food?"

"Right!" Spydie tells you. It starts to laugh, throwing its hideous head back and shaking all over.

"What's so funny?" you ask.

"You!" the monster answers. "You don't even realize that you're turning into a mutant web crawler. Like me. Do you still want to hurt me with that stupid spatula?"

Do you?

Find out on PAGE 7.

You watch, in shock, as Rachel races over to the spider-monster.

She scoops it up and cuddles it!

"I can't believe it's not biting her!" Mark whispers.

He's in awe. So are you.

Rachel comes over, hugging the slimy blue monster and cooing to it.

"He told me that you two were mean to him!" she huffs. "You scared him. That's why he bit you! Now I'm going to make him my pet."

"What about the virus?" you ask. "How do I make it go away?"

Rachel whispers to the Spyder. Then she listens while it croaks an answer.

"He said, 'Just take a hot bubble bath. It'll go away by morning.'"

"Great!" you shout.

"Cool!" Mark yells, giving you a high five.

"Now I'm going to take you home," Rachel coos to her new pet. "I think I'll name you *Web*ster!"

THE END

Congratulations! You're correct.

There are ninety-four words in the E-mail letter.

Hey — maybe you should count the number of words in the whole book. Maybe *that's* the secret number that will help you cure the virus, restore your memory, and zoom you to the happy ending where you save the world from computer viruses!

Yeah. Sure. Right. Start counting. And don't come back here until you get to . . .

THE END.

You've got to make a break for the door.

Your knees are so weak, they're shaking. But you use every ounce of strength to slide off the metal table and push past Dr. Bronstein.

You reach the door and twist the knob.

Locked!

"You're not going anywhere!" Dr. Bronstein roars.

He strides toward you, holding out the biggest, most horrible-looking hypodermic needle you've ever seen.

"No!" you cry. You keep twisting and turning the doorknob, even though you know it's locked.

Keep turning the knob until you reach PAGE 33.

The creatures all have normal human bodies but grotesque monster heads.

"Let's go!" you say urgently. You grab Rachel's arm.

But she bursts out laughing. "Those aren't monsters. They're regular people. But these faces are their screen personalities!"

Huh?

"People don't use their real names on the Internet," Rachel explains between fits of giggling. "They use screen names. It's like a fake personality. So no one will know who they are!"

"I knew that," you mutter. "Well, is your friend here or not?"

Rachel gazes over the crowd of monsters. Even though you know they aren't real, their faces are so hideous they make your flesh crawl.

A grinning skull. A little girl's face with moles sprouting long black hairs. An enormous black gorilla. A giant blue spider-monster.

Wait a minute, you think. A giant spider-monster?

That sounds familiar. . . .

Flip to PAGE 130.

It looks . . . awful!

The plate is full of computer parts. Little electronic chips! Next to the plate is a small bowl of French onion dip.

"Chips and dip!" Dr. Bronstein announces with a smile.

"You've got to be kidding!" you exclaim. "You want me to eat *computer* chips?"

"Trust me," Dr. Bronstein replies. "I know what I'm doing. The only cure for a computer virus is to eat memory chips! They're programmed with virus protection. The onion dip will help them go down easier. *Bon appétit*," he adds.

This sounds crazy. Way *too* crazy.

But what choice do you have? Besides, you're so hungry now, you could eat a whole computer!

You lift a memory chip, scoop up a dab of dip, and take a bite.

If you can swallow that, turn to PAGE 121.

Spydie is attacking the lady! It sinks its pus-covered fangs into her neck.

"Get it off me!" she cries. "Get this thing off me!"

You swat at the monster with a yellow plastic thing you find in your hand.

You miss.

Wait a minute. What were you trying to do?

Spydie laughs. "I warned you," it says. "Your human memory is almost gone now. Soon you'll be a mutant web crawler. You'll do what you're programmed to do. Nothing else."

Huh?

You watch stupidly as Spydie leaps from the lady's shoulder and races to the front door.

A man dressed in a business suit opens the door. "Honey, I'm home — aaaaugh!" he cries as the monster leaps at him and sinks its teeth into his neck.

Spydie races through the front door.

For some reason, you follow it.

Give chase on PAGE 86.

Use bug spray on your computer? No way!

Why ruin thousands of dollars' worth of equipment, when you could just pull the plug?

You race back up to your room. The shrill, screaming beep rattles your brain. You stoop down and reach toward the outlet behind your desk.

You yank the plug out of the outlet.

The noise stops.

Silence. Beautiful silence.

"Phew," you say, letting out a sigh of relief.

You flop down on your bed.

That's when you hear it.

A tiny, muffled voice coming from your computer.

It's calling your name!

But how can that be? You unplugged it!

Find out what it is on PAGE 115.

100

"Unless it went down there." Mark points to the door that leads to the basement. It's slightly ajar.

You gulp.

The basement.

The scariest room in the house. Dark. Dingy. Damp. And filled with choice spots for a big, hairy spider to hide.

"No way," Mark declares.

You roll your eyes. You didn't even ask.

"All right," you say with a sigh. "*I'll* search down there. You keep looking up here."

You try to stop your hand from shaking as you reach for the doorknob.

Descend into the basement on PAGE 122.

"Cool code," you tell Rachel. "But what do we do now?"

"We check out the E-mail that Digit Wizard sent you," Rachel answers. "You'd better take off your VR headset."

You lift the visor off your head. And suddenly you're back in the Peach Pit!

"Phew!" You run a hand through your sweaty hair. "I feel like I've been to the moon," you tell Mark.

"You look like you've been to a grave!" Mark replies. "Your eyes are totally bloodshot. And your tongue . . . whoa! It's turning green! Do you feel okay?"

"Not really," you admit. "But I think we may be on the track of a cure!"

Rachel hurries over to her printer.

"Check this out," she says, handing you the printed copy of the E-mail from Digit Wizard.

Decode the message on PAGE 71.

Dr. Bronstein holds a vial of blood up to the light. "I believe I can use your blood to create a vaccine — a medicine that will protect computers against viruses. No bug will ever infect another computer again!"

"Hold on," you say. "You want to protect *computers*? But what about me? What about curing me?"

"We'll make a lot of money, if it works," Dr. Bronstein says, his eyes twinkling devilishly.

You're about to point out that he hasn't answered your question. But then you stop yourself.

Wait. Did he say *we*? *We* could make a lot of money?

You could *use* a lot of money. You could use it to buy a whole new computer, one without any viruses. And all the latest virus scanners.

Maybe you and Dr. Bronstein need to talk some more!

Try conversing on PAGE 126.

Bad news.

You can't remember the letter writer's name.

Your memory is so fried, you can't even remember your *own* name.

So there's *no way* you're going to remember how to get back to Coffin City to find Rachel!

Face it. You might as well close the book, give your brain a rest, and then start reading at the beginning again — if you can remember how!

THE END

104

No way are you getting into anybody's car! Even for candy. Even if he *does* claim to be your best friend!

Without a word, you turn and run, stumbling your way across the parking lot. You head toward a big patch of trees.

"Wait!" the boy shouts.

This kid just won't quit. He's running after you. Can you make it to the trees and lose him?

Race to PAGE 123.

You manage to lose Crusher by dodging behind an abandoned building. Then you cautiously sneak back to your mailbox. You grab the letter and read it.

It says:

Welcome to your electronic nightmare! I have infected your web crawler with the most powerful virus in the world. Not only will it erase your computer's *memory — it will bite you and erase your brain.*

There is only one cure. Get the web crawler back into the computer — and off the streets.

Of course, I bet you're not smart enough to figure out how to do that.

Which is why you'll probably die. Ha!

If you get really desperate, visit the GOOSEBUMPS website — and search for GOOD LUCK there.

Signed,
Digit Wizard
P.S. ITOEARTSEBAQNAPNAIS

Turn to PAGE 62.

106

The monster, Spyder, explodes like a bursting water balloon.

Steaming gook splatters everywhere.

TSSSSSSSSSS!

You hear a terrible hissing sound as it hits your skin.

And Mark's skin.

And Rachel's.

You thought you had the virus bad *before*!

This stuff stings. And it spreads fast.

You feel sick as you glance down — and see your skin melting before your eyes. This virus makes leprosy seem like a beauty treatment.

Didn't your mother ever teach you not to be so pushy?

THE END

"I can't chase that spider-monster thing. I'm too sick," you tell Rachel and Mark. "Let's go on-line to find a cure."

"Okay." Rachel nods.

"Which computer should we nab?" Mark scans the room, searching for an empty computer station.

Rachel shakes her head. "Not out here," she says. "I have a better place. Come on — I'll show you."

Rachel leads you to a private room at the back of the diner. The room is locked, but she pulls out a key.

"They gave me my own space since I spend so much time here," Rachel explains, unlocking the door. "I call it the Peach Pit."

Wow, you think as you step into Rachel's own private world.

Enter the Peach Pit on PAGE 41.

"No. N-n-not going anywhere," Mark stammers.

But you've had it with this spider. You grab the doorknob and fling open the door, Spydie and all.

You make it as far as the hall.

"Ahhhhhh!" Spydie lets out a war cry and leaps at you. Its legs clamp onto your chest. Its tentacles dig in as if they were cat's claws.

Before you can scream or push it away, Spydie sinks its dripping fangs into your neck.

"Nooooo!" you scream.

The next instant, the monster drops off and scuttles down the stairs.

Scuttle to PAGE 26.

"We've got to try!" You haven't come this far to give up now.

"It's our only chance," Rachel agrees.

Digit Wizard sighs. "Okay. Go home and download the program onto your computer. It's called 'Virus Guard Dog.' It might be able to clean your files. And wipe out the virus at the same time. But I just don't know."

"Let's go!" you shout. "Thanks, Digit," you remember to add.

Is it just your imagination, or do you hear Digit Wizard let out an evil chuckle?

Rachel taps you on the shoulder. "Take off the headset and visor," she orders. "We've got to go back to your house."

You yank off the gear. You, Mark, and Rachel hurry back to your house. Rachel takes over the computer.

She clicks the mouse a few times and finds the file.

"Here it is," Rachel says. "Virus Guard Dog. I'm downloading it now."

Read the download on PAGE 131.

110

"Darling" is a dog.

Not just any dog, either. An enormous Doberman pinscher with rows of razor-sharp teeth.

And it's growling at you.

You gulp as you try to back away. Then something catches your eye. A box.

A glowing box.

It has color pictures! It makes sounds! It's wonderful!

It's TV.

But because your memory is now almost completely fried, it seems totally new to you.

You plop down on the couch and watch the moving pictures. The big dog comes over and sniffs your hand. It yawns and sits at your side.

"Oh! Look!" the lady exclaims. "It's one of my favorite shows. Too bad it's a rerun."

Rerun? What's that?

It's a good thing you don't remember. Because watching reruns is what you're going to do for the rest of your life.

But since you have no memory, they all seem brand-new.

You're very lucky. And this is

THE END.

"Surfing sounds like fun, but I really don't feel *that* well," you explain to Rachel. "The sooner we find this friend of yours — and the antidote — the better. Okay?"

"Sure," Rachel says. "We'll find my friend. Follow me!"

Your feet drag across the marble floor of the lobby as you follow Rachel into a glass elevator. You watch as she presses number 11.

You zoom upward. The doors slide open with a *SHOOSH.* In front of you is a big, open lounge filled with chairs, couches, coffee tables, and people.

"I can't believe how real this all seems," you mumble.

"Yeah! It's pretty cool!" Rachel answers.

As you and Rachel enter the lounge, everyone turns around to check you out. You glimpse their faces — and scream.

"Rachel!" you yell. "Let's get out of here!"

"What's wrong?" Rachel asks.

"Are you kidding?" you sputter. "These people are monsters!"

A werewolf with bloody fangs. A snorting boar with drool-covered tusks. A mummy with rotting flesh!

Face the monsters on PAGE 96.

You, Rachel, and Mark trudge along the street. You're tired. Hot. Sweaty. Achy.

You feel like you're going to die.

"I give up," you moan. "Just put on my tombstone that —"

"There it is!" Mark shouts, interrupting and pointing.

You gulp and freeze.

Scuttling toward you, a block ahead, is the hideous Spyder.

The sight of it, creeping along, makes your heart race.

"I can't believe it!" Rachel whispers. "It's the most . . . the most . . . the most . . ."

". . . hideous, disgusting thing you've ever seen!" You finish her sentence for her.

"No!" Rachel cries. "That's not it at all! I think it's the *cutest* thing I've ever seen!"

"What?" you gasp. Shocked.

"Are you crazy?" Mark shouts.

Rachel rushes toward the monster.

"Rachel!" you cry. "Nooooooo!"

Race to PAGE 93.

After a horrible second, you realize the kid was wearing a mask. Underneath is a face with freckles and long red hair.

It's a girl. Have you met her before?

"Don't try escaping again," she warns you. She gives you a kick in the side. "We won't be so gentle next time. Right, Dad?"

"Be nice, Rachel," the bearded guy says. "It was worth the trouble. We need a human kid infected with the Spyder virus."

Spyder virus?

The bearded guy gazes at you. He chuckles. "In only a few months, you'll turn into a mutant web crawler."

Mutant? Sounds bad. But you're too weak to care.

The guy and his daughter hoist you into their van. They drive you back to their lab.

At least you're getting regular meals now. Interesting meals. Your favorite one is this pudding made of ground-up computer chips and tiny black flies.

Dr. Bronstein and his daughter, Rachel — the humans who train you — say that spring is coming soon. You're glad. In spring you'll finally get a chance to crawl the World Wide Web. That's all you'll do, from now on. Crawl the Web, obey the doctor. Forever.

You can hardly wait.

THE END

"Home," you decide. "Definitely."

"I'm just going to bring some equipment, in case we need it," Rachel says. She loads a scanner, a digital notepad, and some other stuff into a backpack.

"Let's go!" Mark shouts.

You, Mark, and Rachel race out of the diner. You stop to buy some bananas on the way.

When you get home, you spread the bananas around the house. Three on the floor by the front door. Two on the stairs leading up to your room. Three more by the kitchen door. Five on the dining room table.

You can't stop glancing over your shoulder. Every shadow makes you jump. Your nerves are totally jangled.

Because the monster, Spyder, could be anywhere.

"Now all we can do is wait," Mark says.

At that moment a noisy, slurping, munching sound comes from the dining room.

ULP!

Tiptoe into the dining room on PAGE 8.

You sit up fast, your heart pounding as you approach your computer.

Slowly. Very slowly.

The tiny voice gets louder. It calls your name again.

You glance out the window by your desk — and do a double take.

It's Mark! He's standing in your backyard, waving and calling up to you!

And you thought it was the computer!

Laughing at your mistake, you raise the window. "Hey, Mark!" you yell. "I unplugged it and the beeping stopped! You can come back in." You grin. "That is . . . if you're not too scared!"

Mark kicks sheepishly at the dirt.

"Okay," he says.

Go on up to PAGE 19.

116

You catch the next wave and the next. You're so focused you don't hear Rachel nagging you to get back.

Hours go by.

Finally, you feel someone snatch the virtual reality gear off your face.

"Hey! Who did that?" You stare blankly at a tall, red-headed girl. "Who are you, anyway?"

"Oh, brother," a wavy-haired kid standing next to the girl moans out loud. "Total lobotomy."

"Yup," the girl agrees, shaking her head. "No brains left at all."

The boy leads you home. He introduces you to some people he calls your parents. He tells them a long, confusing story about spider-monsters and computer viruses.

The parents show you to a computer station and leave you sitting there. You stare at the monitor for days on end. You can't remember what it's for. Though every now and then you get the urge to wrap it in a shimmering spiderweb. You love crawling on the Web!

THE END

You decide to start walking.

Maybe you'll recognize something — or someone.

Or maybe . . . just maybe . . . someone will recognize you!

Every time you pass a stranger on the street, you gaze into the person's eyes. Hopefully. Desperately.

Do you know me? you want to say. Was I a friend of yours — before my memory was erased?

But no one even notices you.

Keep walking to PAGE 91.

118

Forget the stupid E-mail, you decide.

You want out of this Internet nightmare.

You reach up to yank off the virtual reality goggles and headset.

"Mark?" you say as you lift the goggles. "Where did you go?"

YIKES!

You expected to be back in the Peach Pit the instant you removed the goggles. With Mark sitting in the chair. And Rachel standing right beside you.

But instead . . .

Turn to PAGE 31.

You dash into the dining room. Mark and Rachel are right behind you.

What's the worst that can happen? you're thinking. It's already bitten you, right?

Just as you're gathering your courage to grab the thing, it hurls itself at your face.

Your eyes. Your mouth. Your nose. They're covered by the Spyder's giant, gooey body.

You can't breathe!

Turn to PAGE 134.

120

"It's the letter!" you shout at Rachel. "The E-mail letter from Digit Wizard. I'll bet there's a clue — in the number of words, or something. Computer programmers love math puzzles, right?"

"You mean, maybe if we count the number of words, it'll be a code that will help us break the virus?" Rachel asks.

"Something like that," you answer.

Rachel shrugs. "Okay," she says. "Go ahead and count them."

Go ahead. Do it.

Turn back to page 105. Count the number of words in the E-mail letter, including the signature. Count the last line of the letter as two words.

Turn to the page with the same number as the number of words in the letter.

The chip goes down incredibly smoothly. Wow!

"Not bad at all," you announce. "These are great! You ought to try them."

"Me? Oh, no, no," Dr. Bronstein laughs. "I can't eat those. I'm entirely human. But you've been bitten by an infected web crawler. You're part web crawler. From now on, these chips are your only food. And the best part is, eating them will restore your memory."

"Really?" You suddenly realize that your fever is gone. And your aches and pains. "Wow! Wait till I tell Mark," you say, grinning because you remembered his name.

Your brain is fixed!

You give yourself another serving, wondering if your mom can learn to cook computer parts.

Like, chocolate chip chips . . . chipped beef chips . . . nacho chip chips . . .

Bon appétit!

THE END

The basement is dark. Even after you flip on the light. There's only one dim, flickering bulb in a corner.

CREAK! CREAK! The stairs moan as you step down them.

Something soft brushes against your neck. You jump about a mile, screaming your head off.

Then you realize it's only an old mop. You stop screaming, but you realize someone *else* is screaming now.

Mark!

You bound back up the stairs into the kitchen.

"It bit me!" Mark cries. With one hand, he's holding closed the door to the cabinet under the sink.

He holds out his other hand, showing you an ugly, swollen, red bite mark on his wrist. Bits of yellow pus cling to it.

"Let me out!" Spydie's growling voice comes through the door. "Let me out and I'll give you something you need!"

Find out what Spydie wants to give you on PAGE 129.

You made it! You shoot into the patch of woods and crouch down behind a big oak tree. Panting and out of breath.

You're in no shape for this! By now you're sick as a dog.

Which is why you don't hear the guy who's sneaking up on you from behind.

Suddenly you feel something draping over you. A net! You struggle frantically, but the net just tightens around you. You lose your balance and crash to the ground.

You twist your head painfully and peer through the mesh. You catch sight of a tall man with a beard.

Silently, he drags you back to the green van.

The kid is there. Waiting.

You were right not to trust him! you think to yourself as something really weird happens. Something really awful.

The kid reaches up and pulls off his face!

Eek! Turn to PAGE 113.

A sticky silvery thread is shooting out of your mouth.

You're shooting spider silk!

You must be mutating! Turning into a spider! Disgusting!

Though, come to think of it, spider silk is pretty strong stuff. Great for tying up victims.

Now, how do you tie up Crusher?

Part of your brain must be programmed to do spider stuff. Because in the next instant, Crusher is spinning around as you wrap him in an endless cocoon of spider thread.

"Let me go!" Crusher shouts. "This isn't part of the game!"

You ignore him. Soon Crusher's arms are pinned to his sides. He's totally helpless.

You reach into the grave and help Rachel climb out.

"That was *way* cool!" Rachel declares with a grin.

It was, wasn't it?

Maybe being part mutant spider isn't so bad after all.

"Hey," Rachel says. "Now that Crusher's helpless, let's have some fun!"

Go have fun on PAGE 82.

"It's for flipping pancakes!" you shout. Proudly. You *do* remember!

"Whom are you talking to, dear?" a voice behind you asks.

You spin around. A nice lady is coming in the back door with a bag of groceries in each hand.

What's her name again? Mop? Moll? Mob?

It's on the tip of your tongue. . . .

But before you can come up with it, the nice lady opens her mouth and lets out a horrible, bloodcurdling scream.

She won't stop screaming until you turn to PAGE 98.

"Tell me more about this plan," you ask the doctor. "Can you cure me with this vaccine?"

"Oh, no," Dr. Bronstein answers. "I need your infected blood to make the vaccine. But don't worry," he adds. "The only problem you'll have is a slight loss of memory. Computer viruses can erase small bits of memory, you know."

You didn't know. But you think about it. Hard.

So you won't remember some arithmetic. Or history.

So how big a deal is that?

"Okay," you agree. "Use my blood to make the vaccine. As long as we share all the money you make!"

"Of course," Dr. Bronstein agrees. He takes a bit more blood and begins work.

You move in with him and his daughter, Rachel. Within a year, you become rich. Or at least, you think you're rich. Didn't the doctor tell you so?

You can't quite remember what he tells you. For that matter, you can't quite remember where you used to live. Or who you were. Or if you ever wanted to do anything but lie here and give more blood . . . more blood . . . more blood. . . .

THE END

The Spyder pulls out of your grip.

Mark is still trying to hold on. "Hurry!" he cries.

"I scanned it in!" Rachel shouts. She clicks your mouse frantically, over and over. "But it won't delete. Your hard drive is too slow!"

"No!" Mark shouts as the creature breaks free and dashes for the door.

Which is open.

"Slam it!" you scream. "Close the door!"

Go on to PAGE 132.

You gaze at the big yellow house. At the red roses growing by the front door. It looks so warm and inviting.

"Why not knock on the door?" you say out loud. "I mean, nice people might live there. They could help. Anyway, it can't be any worse than what's already happened. I've been bitten by a spider-monster that crawled out of my *computer*! And I'm losing my memory!"

Uh-oh. You're also talking to yourself!

Knock on that door fast — before things get *really* out of hand!

Knock your way to PAGE 21.

"Pretty please?" Spydie's voice grows softer. Gentler. "If you let me out — I'll tell you how to treat the virus!"

Hmmm. Maybe you should let the ugly thing out. . . .

But what if it's a trick?

To let Spydie out, turn to PAGE 47.

To keep the monster under the sink, turn to PAGE 25.

130

"Hey, Rachel!" You nudge her. "Who's that person wearing the four-eyed spider-monster mask?"

"Never seen him before," she replies. She turns to you. "My friend's not here. Come on. Let's go search another floor."

Something tells you the kid with the spider-monster head would know about the web crawler, Spyder, who jumped out of your screen.

"Come on," Rachel repeats, pulling your arm. What do you do?

To talk to the Spyder-kid, turn to PAGE 76.
To stay with Rachel and try to find her friend, turn to PAGE 44.

For a moment your screen goes crazy. Colors and numbers flash across it like lightning.

Then a message appears. It says:

YOUR VIRUS IS GONE. I HAVE EATEN IT. BUT I'M STILL HUNGRY.

FEED ME NOW — OR EXPERIENCE A FATAL ERROR.

Uh-oh. Hasn't this all happened before?

"Feed it?" you wail. "Feed it what?"

Before Mark or Rachel can answer, an ugly beast of a dog appears on your screen. And the screen begins to bulge!

"GGRRRRRRRRR!"

As it tears its way out of the monitor, the dog becomes monster-size.

"He tricked us!" Rachel cries. "Digit Wizard tricked us!"

"RRRUUFFFF! GRRRRRRRR!"

The dog opens its mouth wider than you thought possible.

You're about to learn the real meaning of the word *megabyte*!

THE END

Mark lunges. He slams the door shut.

Just in time. The Spyder is trapped in your room.

Rachel clicks the mouse a few more times. "Got it!" she cries triumphantly.

You glance at the Spyder.

Then you stare, jaw hanging open.

The creature has almost completely vanished. It is being wiped away, from bottom to top, just as the computer graphic is being erased from your screen.

You catch a final glimpse of the last blue tentacle before it disappears.

Whoa!

"Is it really gone?" you ask.

Turn to PAGE 66.

"Curing the virus is easy," Spydie says between guffaws. "But you won't like it!"

"Why not?" you ask.

"You have to make a special soup," the monster answers. "Cook up pig's knuckles, fish heads, sheep's eyeballs, and Brussels sprouts. And add some computer chips."

You and Mark glance at each other. Your eyes lock.

No way, your expressions say.

"You've got to eat four gallons of it," Spydie goes on. "Every day. For a week."

No possible way.

"I'd rather be a walking zombie than eat that stuff," Mark declares.

"Yeah!" you agree. "I'd rather . . . I'd rather . . ."

But you can't finish the sentence.

You've forgotten how to speak!

You should have jumped at the chance to eat that disgusting soup. Because now you're in serious trouble.

You've forgotten how to eat as well!

For you, and for Mark, this is

THE END.

Rachel and Mark help you grab the awful thing and pull.

THWOPPPPP!

With a ripping sound, like a giant suction cup letting go, the Spyder releases its grip.

"Ugh! Now what do we do with it?" Rachel asks as the monster squirms violently.

"Bring it upstairs!" you shout.

You stumble up the stairs to your room. You all have a hold on the wriggling monster, keeping it as far from your bodies as possible.

"We-we-we could try to scan it back into the computer with my scanner," Rachel stammers.

"No! Let's just shove it back in through the screen!" Mark yells. "That's the way it came out!"

To scan the giant Spyder into your computer, turn to PAGE 42.

To shove it into the monitor, turn to PAGE 90.

"I'll go get Rachel," Mark tells you. "Stay there, okay?"

You nod weakly.

Mark hurries to the back corner to talk to Rachel.

A few minutes later, the two of them return and sit down beside you.

"I told her everything," Mark explains. "About the messages on your screen, and the bulge, and the spider-monster. And how it bit you, and how you can't remember stuff."

"You look really sick," Rachel comments. She shakes her head, staring at you as if you're a cooked goose.

"What? You can't help me?" you ask.

"I can," Rachel says. "But it's going to be tricky. We've got two choices. We could try to catch the monster. Then maybe I could dissect it. Or we can go into the Internet and look for a cure. I think I might know how to find an antidote."

There are three of you now. Maybe you should try to find the thing that bit you.

Then again, an antidote sounds really good!

Quick! Make up your mind!

To go out looking for the Spyder, turn to PAGE 79.

To surf the Net for a cure for the virus, turn to PAGE 107.

About R.L. Stine

R.L. Stine is the most popular author in America. He is the creator of the *Goosebumps, Give Yourself Goosebumps, Fear Street,* and *Ghosts of Fear Street* series, among other popular books. He has written more than 250 scary novels for kids. Bob lives in New York City with his wife, Jane, teenage son, Matt, and dog, Nadine.

Log on for Scares!

Scholastic presents

Goosebumps

ON THE WEB!

http://www.scholastic.com/goosebump

- The latest books!
- Really gross recipes!
- Exclusive contests!
- Start your own Goosebumps reading club!
- How to get Goosebumps stuff: sportswear, CD-ROMs, video releases and more!
- Author R.L. Stine's tips on writing!
- Craft ideas!
- Interactive word games and activities!